MRJC
4/15

D0777408

GRIMSTONES

MORTIMER REVEALED

by Asphyxia

the second magnificently secret diary of Martha Grimstone

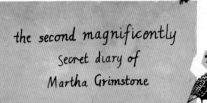

ALLEN&UNWIN

SYDNEY • MELBOURNE • AUCKLAND • LONDON

First published in 2012

Copyright © Asphyxia 2012

All rights reserved. No part of this book may
be reproduced or transmitted in any form
or by any means, electronic or mechanical,
including photocopying, recording or by any
information storage and retrieval system,
without prior permission in writing from the
publisher. The *Australian Copyright Act 1968*
(the Act) allows a maximum of one chapter
or ten per cent of this book, whichever is the
greater, to be photocopied by any educational
institution for its educational purposes
provided that the educational institution
(or body that administers it) has given a
remuneration notice to Copyright Agency
Limited (CAL) under the Act.

Allen & Unwin
83 Alexander Street
Crows Nest NSW 2065
Australia
Phone: (61 2) 8425 0100
Fax: (61 2) 9906 2218
Email: info@allenandunwin.com
Web: www.allenandunwin.com

A Cataloguing-in-Publication entry is available
from the National Library of Australia
www.trove.nla.gov.au

ISBN 978 1 74237 689 9

Cover and text design by Jenine Davidson
Cover photograph by Taras Mohamed
Set in 11 pt Bookman Old Style by Jenine Davidson
Internal photographs by Asphyxia,
Adis Hondo (www.handinhand.com.au) and
Taras Mohamed (www.tarasmohamed.com)
Artwork by Asphyxia, Jenine Davidson and Jesse Dowse
This book was printed in December 2013 at
Everbest Printing Co Ltd in 334 Huanshi Road South,
Nansha, Guangdong, China.

3 5 7 9 10 8 6 4 2

THE GRIMSTONES

Created & written
by Asphyxia

Designed and typeset by Jenine Davidson

Big Ideas, especially for story
and characters, by Kelly Parry

Photographs by Adis Hondo,
Taras Mohamed
and Asphyxia

Illustrations by Asphyxia,
Jenine Davidson and Jesse Dowse

Fantastic editing by Rosalind Price,
Eva Mills and Elise Jones

Encouragement and spots of inspiration
by Paula Dowse and Jesse Dowse

General holding-together of everything,
especially sanity, by Roe Ritchie

www.thegrimstones.com

MONDAY

My Dear Diary,

I'm writing this under the mulberry tree as I watch Crumpet play. When I say under the tree, I mean I'm hanging upside down with my knees hooked over a crooked branch. I'm learning to write like this, so you'll have to forgive my messy script until I get the hang of it (ha ha!).

I'm clinking my shoes together in time to the rustling of the leaves, and humming the mulberry tune I invented. The leaves are curling and brown at the edges, even though they are new springtime leaves. I stroke the mulberry's trunk and wish I could give her an enormous drink of water so she could grow pretty green leaves. This is one of my very favourite places –

along with the creek and the attic.

Oh no! Crumpet's climbed to the very top of the tree, and he's too young for that. Having three legs makes him a good climber, but he's not so good at holding on because he has only two arms. And now he's dangling from the highest branch! Should I drop my journal and execute my Most Magnificent Lady of the Sky-Circus flip so I can catch him as he falls?

But phew – no need! At the very moment Crumpet's fingers gave way, there was a *pfft* of wind and he floated gently to the ground, all by himself. He chuckles, shoving a fistful of mulberries into his mouth.

Crumpet finds a touch of magic at every turn. If it were me, I'd be a splat-shaped puddle on the ground, and the bird that follows me everywhere would dive in and steal one of my plaits to build the grandest bird's nest ever seen in this valley!

Dear me, I'm jumping ahead. I meant to introduce myself properly, now that I have a new journal to write in, but Crumpet distracted me – as usual. I am Martha Grimstone, sometimes known as Lady Martha the Magnificent, or the Magnificent Lady of the Upside-down Writing Act, and Crumpet is my baby brother. Due to a slight mishap before his birth, which may or may not have been my fault, Crumpet will never grow up. So it's my responsibility to look after him, but that's easy, because I adore him.

Crumpet has the gift of magic – a gift I wish I had myself. I haven't given up on finding my own magical talents, though – I believe they're lurking just below the surface, even if no one else believes it, except maybe Crumpet.

When I'm not in the mulberry tree, I live with my family in a big old house built by my great-great-great-great-great-great (something like that) grandparents.

The bird – which didn't get my plait.

It's awfully grand, even though you see things that need fixing everywhere you look.

Such as our poor weathervane, all cracked from the heat – which I'd best go and attend to now, so I will tell you more about our home another time, my papery new friend.

MONDAY

On the landing in our home sits the old doll's house. It's been there for as long as I can remember. I've played with it once or twice, but honestly, I think dolls are a bit boring. So it's sat there for years gathering dust and cobwebs, until this morning, when Crumpet poked open the front door and peered inside. His face lit up with delight.

'Izzzt,' he said, and I could see the dolls lined up in the parlour, their clothes faded and dirty.

I unlatched the front and opened it up to reveal all the rooms inside. The doll's house is exactly like our house, but smaller, built long ago by one of my Grimstone ancestors. Upstairs on the left is a perfect miniature version of the bedroom I share with Mama and Crumpet. In the middle is the landing, with a doll-sized rocking horse and tiny chest of toys. To the right is a sewing room just like Mama's, only far neater. Where she has fabric and threads and buttons all over the floor, the doll's house has neat baskets of cotton spools, jars of teeny pearls, and piles of velvety fabric.

Below the sewing room is the kitchen, with its wood stove, hanging copper pots, and even a tiny wooden rolling pin on the workbench.

Next to the kitchen is the dining room, then the parlour, and then the apothecary – my very favourite room. The miniature version looks just like the real one; even the labels on the jars, titles on the books, and row of herbs strung from the ceiling are the same. If only I could shrink myself down and make the doll's house apothecary my workspace. There'd be no Grandpa Grimstone to send me away then.

At the very top of the doll's house is an attic, same as in our house, only the miniature one simply has a pair of wooden chests while ours is crammed with boxes, crates, broken furnishings, clothes, jars and spiders. There was only one spider in the doll's house this morning, and it scuttled away as I unlatched the front. 'It's all right,' I reassured it. 'We won't play for long.'

'Izzzt,' Crumpet said again, pointing.

There is a doll that looks just like my Aunt Gertrude, with a black ruffled taffeta dress and a sinister net over her hair. If this doll could talk, she would probably order me to count all those teensy pearls in the sewing room and use them to solve a complex equation as a maths exercise.

Then there's another far prettier doll, with a lovely crinoline dress and roses in her hair. Secretly I call her Velvetta, after my very own mama.

There's a scruffy gardener doll (I've always called him August) wearing dirty overalls and a tiny checked shirt with patches on its sleeves.

The father doll has short black hair, a dapper moustache, and an elegant suit. He doesn't look like my father, but I call him Mortimer anyway. The real Mortimer Grimstone died when I was a baby. I don't remember him, and I don't know if he even loved me at all, for no one will talk about him.

There's an old-man doll who reminds me of Grandpa Grimstone, and a grandma doll, too. I have no grandmother, so I don't know what to call her, but I like the look of her very much.

And then there are two children dolls. The one I like best is the little girl with black plaits and a navy-blue pleated dress. She reminds me of myself, and yet she is not me.

The grandfather clock really works ... and —
always shows the correct time (even though
no one winds it!)

See how pretty the Mama doll is.

There are no little-boy dolls with three legs – but Crumpet didn't seem disappointed. 'Eplgh,' he said, and the grandma doll rose, walked woodenly up the stairs, and settled in the sewing room to hand-stitch a cloth. I could hardly believe my eyes!

'Pffrgh,' said Crumpet, and the Aunt Gertrude doll went stiffly into the kitchen and began cooking, while the Grandpa Grimstone doll moved to the apothecary and stirred the cauldron, just as my grandpa was doing in real life at that very moment.

(Today Grandpa Grimstone had to boil devil-snake eyeballs as part of a potion to heal Rosie Johnson's indigestion. I offered to track the temperature with the Thermomenator, but he wouldn't allow it. Hmph.)

I pointed at the girl doll with black plaits. 'Do her,' I begged Crumpet, who thankfully says no to me far less often than Grandpa Grimstone does.

'Frrrrp.' The black-plaits doll climbed the stairs and sat on the rocking horse, tilting it back and forwards. I was disappointed. Couldn't she do something more adventurous?

Crumpet quickly said, 'Rgghp.' This time Miss Black Plaits turned a cartwheel, revealing tiny white bloomers under her dress. Then she slid down the stair banister on her stomach, landing on her face on the floor. I laughed and Crumpet made a loud gurgling sound, which is his way of laughing.

'More!'

Crumpet thought for a moment, then grinned at me, rubbing two of his feet together mischievously. 'Dwfppp.'

The Aunt Gertrude doll went into the parlour and took the hands of the August doll; then they started dancing together! They danced closer and closer, until the August doll wrapped his arms around the Aunt Gertrude doll's waist, bent her right back, and leaned down to kiss her. I didn't know whether to be delighted or horrified. Aunt Gertrude must never see this! His lips were about to touch hers when...

'Oh! You're playing with the doll's house!' It was Mama, clearly pleased to see us using this old toy.

The dolls sprang apart, landing on the floor with a wooden *clunk*. The Grandpa Grimstone doll froze mid-stir, and the grandma doll paused with her needle in the cloth.

Mama crouched down and peered into the

house. She picked up Miss Black Plaits and smoothed her dress. 'This one reminds me of you, Martha.' She tottered her into the sewing room to sit beside the grandma doll.

Well, this astonished me more than anything Crumpet had done with the dolls, for I have never in my life seen Mama *play* with anything – except Crumpet.

But here she was,

sitting with us as though she were the kind of mama who plays with dolls all the time, instead of the kind who sews exquisite garments late into the night as she grieves for my dead father.

Crumpet reached for the Velvetta doll. 'Who is that?' I asked Mama.

'These are dolls from the Grimstone family long, long ago, so I don't know their names. After all, I wasn't a Grimstone until I married your father.'

And that's another odd thing. Mama said the words 'your father' without obvious distress. She picked up the dapper man doll. 'This one doesn't look like Mortimer at all. Mortimer didn't have a moustache.' Now her voice did catch, a little, and she swallowed hard. A single tear ran down her cheek.

Mama placed the man doll in the sewing room next to the Velvetta doll and straightened up. 'I'll leave you to it. I must see if the fabric for Mr Sterling's coat has arrived.' She dabbed her cheek with her handkerchief and swept down the stairs.

'Let's make a storm!' I said to Crumpet when she'd gone. 'And you can get the Grandpa doll to fight it with a special brew.'

Our valley is often attacked by terrible storms that damage the village and destroy the herbs Grandpa Grimstone needs for his magic potions.

'Kzzzzch,' Crumpet said, and the Grandpa doll sprung to life again, pouring special ingredients into the cauldron, opening and closing books to check their secrets. The other dolls came to life, too, and trooped into the parlour – which is where we hide when there's a real storm, for it's the safest room in the house.

'We need some weather,' I suggested.

Crumpet frowned. 'Glph.' Nothing happened. 'Qwrrk.' Still nothing. 'Ep.' Nothing. He turned his big eyes on me and shrugged.

'I'll have to do it myself,' I said, and rattled the house. The dolls fell over, then stood themselves up again.

Crumpet leaned closer and blew hard, as if blowing out a birthday candle. But all he managed was a feeble breeze, not enough for a storm.

Just then, the bird flew in to the landing. She perched on the chimney of the doll's house and stared at us with her sharp, beady eyes. Then she spread her wings out wide and beat them hard, making the house rock. The dolls grasped the furniture, which slid around the parlour. The Grandpa doll waved his hands over the cauldron, bringing out a coil of green smoke. Suddenly there was a small explosion of blue sparks from the cauldron and the Grandpa doll fell over. The house crashed against the landing wall, and the bird flew off in fright. Crumpet grinned. 'Rwdhh,' he said, which I took to mean, 'There – Grandpa fixed the storm.'

'MARTHA GRIMSTONE!'

Aunt Gertrude's voice suddenly boomed up the stairs. 'I'm expecting you for your lessons.'

I sighed. Lessons with Aunt Gertrude are the most tedious part of my day. If only I could spend that time learning something more interesting than Latin and long division, such as how to use magic to ward off a storm in real life.

WEDNESDAY

Aunt Gertrude usually sits with me at the kitchen table for my lessons; while I complete the tasks she's set me, she goes through household receipts, prepares orders for things we need, and writes out bills for people who've bought garments or medicines from us. Today, however, Aunt Gertrude stood at the kitchen bench surrounded by apples.

'You must set your own course of study today, Martha, for the cider requires my attention.'

Crumpet crawled across the kitchen floor and dipped into a box of apples, rolling the fruit this way and that. We've been eating the apples all winter, bringing up a new box from the cellar every week. But now it's warmer we have mulberries to eat,

and Aunt Gertrude has to turn all the leftover apples into cider before they spoil.

I grinned, opened my workbook, and began choreographing a synchronised-swimming performance for the fish that live in the creek. I had written the first two symbols of my special choreography notation when:

I spun around to find Aunt Gertrude wielding a marble chopping board. She was using it to smack the apples on the bench, hoping to squish them.

'This situation is preposterous!' she exclaimed. 'It will take an age to crush all these apples!' She whacked the fruit again.

I put my fingers in my ears and was doing my best to concentrate on my fish dance when I spotted August's anxious face at the kitchen window. Aunt Gertrude saw him too, and shouted, 'You! Back to work!'

Grandpa Grimstone chose that very moment to walk through the door. 'Why, Gertrude, I've been working all morning. That's not very courteous of you.'

Aunt Gertrude snorted in what some may describe as quite an unladylike fashion, and smashed another apple. Grandpa Grimstone ignored her, scooping Crumpet onto his hip and shucking his cheek. 'Shall we go and check on the sneef-pods?' Crumpet wriggled with delight and they disappeared around the kitchen door.

And now, you might ask, where is Grandpa Grimstone taking Crumpet? This is the part of my day that is **SO UNFAIR** it makes my blood swell up into huge bubbles that **POP LOUDLY!**

Grandpa came to fetch Crumpet for *his* lessons! Yes – it's true. Crumpet has his own lessons to do. Grandpa Grimstone has recognised Crumpet's gift of magic and decided he must be trained in the magical arts from an early age.

'Train ME in the magical arts!' I begged him the first time he fetched Crumpet.

'Martha dear, you lack this particular gift. You must accept the things you can and can't do, just as Crumpet must accept his own talents and limitations.'

'I DO NOT LACK THIS PARTICULAR GIFT!'

I shouted, so cross that I started to turn a bit deaf from all the blood explosions. And I gestured to Crumpet, the ultimate proof that I *can* work magic – REAL, SERIOUS magic. But that's another story, and you'll have to read about it in my first diary.

Grandpa Grimstone stared very pointedly at Crumpet's three legs, and then he swept out of the room, carrying Crumpet with him.

And that is what he has proceeded to do every day since – including today.

I gave up on my fish choreography after that, and instead started writing in you, Dear Diary. Aunt Gertrude is so frustrated by her cider-apple battle that she hasn't even noticed I'm not doing my work.

THURSDAY

Today a terrible storm blew through our valley, so we took shelter in the parlour. Grandpa Grimstone mixed and stirred his magical concoctions, calling out incantations to the sky:

'... of aleutian low
    galeo trans meridian
  precipitate to Northern aphelion
    quasi-mercurial nadir
      azores atmospheric
        dispatch castellanus
     via celestial perehelion ...'

'At least the storm should bring rain,' August said. 'The curly leafed streffon is so parched that it's coiled itself down into the earth to conserve moisture.'

Springtime is usually the wettest season, but this year we haven't had a single drop of rain. Our

whole valley is brown. The Emmersons' cows are so thin they haven't given milk for weeks, and the fish in the creek have been flopping miserably by the rocks, as there's not enough water for them to dance in. (Naturally my new choreography consists entirely of shallow-water moves.)

Today, even as the wind hurled against the windows, the sky split with lightning, and the house shook with rumbles of thunder, not one drop of rain fell. Instead, a tree crashed down against the parlour window, smashing the glass. We all jumped, and wind whipped our faces as we scrambled into the hall.

'Oh damnation – I mean *bother*,' Aunt Gertrude said as the parlour door slammed shut behind us and we stood shivering in the dark hall. 'We cannot possibly rectify this inopportune development!'

By which she meant: 'This is unfortunate, as we can't afford a new pane of glass.'

'Mr Sterling has ordered a new suit,' Mama said softly. 'He'll pay us handsomely for that.'

'But do you envision you can complete it in time for the solstice?' Aunt Gertrude asked anxiously.

Once a year, on the summer solstice, we host a

party for the villagers. This is a tradition from long ago, when the Grimstone mansion was a fine, stately home. It was to treat villagers to hearty food and give them an occasion to dress in their best gowns. Nowadays there's nothing fine or stately about our home, and we are just as poor as the villagers – probably poorer. But we keep up the tradition, as while they're here half the villagers confide their ills and ailments in Grandpa Grimstone and he sells all sorts of potions; the other half admire the beautiful clothing Mama's stitched, ordering a new dress or a coat for next winter. We live for most of the year on the orders made during the solstice.

But we cannot possibly host a grand solstice party with a boarded-up window in the parlour.

'It should be ready well before then,' Mama said.

Aunt Gertrude nodded. 'As long as we've no more breakages.'

I peered through the foyer window and watched as a fence post was hurled into the letterbox, splintering it into a hundred pieces.

At the very same moment there was an enormous crash and the sound of glass shattering above us. We all glanced up, but the only thing we could see in the gloom was the ceiling.

Aunt Gertrude sighed. 'Yet another misfortune.'

FRIDAY

This morning, I dealt with the second misfortune.
I am particularly pleased with our new letterbox:

letters
in
here

What do you think?
I like it so much that when
I'm grown up I shall build one
just like it, only larger, for
Crumpet and me to live in.

This afternoon, August climbed the ladder to the attic to deal with the third misfortune. Crumpet and I followed. At least it won't matter much if the attic window's boarded up; it'll just make the house look a little less grand, which it does every year anyway.

August started sweeping the broken glass into a pile. I listened to the delicate tinkle as the fragments of glass spun across the floor like a cascade of diamonds. 'Da dum! Da da da dummm...' I sang, making up a pretty tune to go with it, my heels rattling against the floor. Even the regular **WHACKS** that floated up from the kitchen suddenly sounded musical as I kept time with them.

'Kmmfch,' said Crumpet, and I looked up to find him astride a red velvet seat, holding on to straps of leather as if they were reins.

'Giddy up!' I said, and he pretended to gallop. The seat was an odd thing – its leg was like the ornate heel of a lady's shoe.

Crumpet was surrounded by a pile of curious objects. 'What are these?' I asked August.

He peered at the collection. 'Oh, that would be one of Mortimer's piles of odds and ends. He was always crafting the most peculiar things.'

My heart sprouted little wings of excitement. 'What sorts of things did he make?'

brass crossbow –thingy

bone pegs

knobs with curious markings

BISSELL'S JUNIOR

August nailed a board across the gaping hole that had been the window. 'I'm not too sure, Miss Martha. He was older than me, always being learned by your grandfather. Else he was off tinkering about somewhere. I was a bit afeared of his cleverness, in truth. It wasn't like we was close. You really ought to ask Velvetta.'

I thought of my father's pale, waxy hands and tried to imagine them tinkering about with something.

I have a secret to tell you, one I've never told anyone, even Crumpet... but I know I can trust you with this, Dear Diary. Sometimes I visit my father in his crypt. And when I say 'visit', I mean I actually open the grave and look inside. Don't worry, it's all right: Grandpa Grimstone has put a potion inside his body so he doesn't decay. Without this, he'd be crawling with maggots and his body would have returned to the earth long ago. Instead, my father lies there day in and day out, cold and covered with cobwebs. My family never speaks of him, and I know almost nothing about him.

It's difficult to imagine him alive, breathing and moving about, collecting piles of odds and ends

R.I.P.

in loving Memory

of

Mortimer
Grimstone

and turning them into unspecified objects.

Crumpet hammered his fist against a handsome wooden chest I'd never seen before to get my attention. August had moved it to the floor when he was clearing a path to the window.

'Yes, yes, I'll open it,' I told Crumpet.

I heaved the lid up and we both peered inside. A deep mustiness rose to meet us. At first I was disappointed, for on top was an ordinary quilt, but underneath we found folds of the softest, silkiest fabric I've ever seen. 'Grvv,' said Crumpet, squeezing a fistful of it in his palm.

Suddenly the fabric stirred, lifted itself out of Crumpet's hand, and shook itself into a dress. I heard the *chink* of glasses, and smelled the spicy tang of warm cider. The dress twirled and a leather glove fell to the floor. The dust morphed into the shape of a girl a little older than me, with two dark plaits, dancing inside the dress. Then the image faded, the dress crumpled to the floor, and all I could smell was damp.

'That was the girl from the doll's house!' I cried to Crumpet. 'Did you show me the past? It looked like a summer solstice party from long ago.'

Crumpet gurgled loudly and nodded, and a thought flew into my head – a big, amazing, ⚡ELECTRIFYING thought.

I grasped Crumpet by the shoulders. 'You know past-revealing magic! Is that what Grandpa Grimstone has been teaching you? Then you can show me my father! You *must*, Crumpet, you *must*!'

Crumpet wriggled free and crawled backwards a few paces. He pointed at the dress.

'You need a dress belonging to Mortimer? Well, all right, not a dress, but a piece of his clothing? Or just something that belonged to him? This?' I pointed to the pile of odds and ends.

But Crumpet shrugged, and no matter what I asked him, he couldn't tell me any more. I drummed my feet against the floor, trying not to scream with frustration.

August meanwhile had finished the window and was enthusiastically filling his pockets with bits and bobs from a chest on the other side of the attic. 'Miss Martha,' he called over to me, 'I've an idea…which might just be to Miss Gertrude's liking.' He held up a silver teapot and a large ornate horn.

But I barely heard what he'd said – for my mind was whirling with the idea there may be a magic that could answer the four thousand and thirty-two questions I have about my dead father!

August

MONDAY

After my lessons today I went to find Mama, the keeper of great secrets. If only I had the right key, I'd unlock her mind and find out everything she knows.

She was perched on a footstool in her sewing room, reaching for a pile of fabrics on the top shelf.

'Martha!' she said. 'Do give me a hand, sweetheart. I know there's just the right thing up here to line Mr Sterling's jacket: a cream silk with tiny blue diamonds on it. Stand back against that wall and see if you can see it.'

I moved the mannequin so I could stand in just the right spot. 'A little to the left. No, not that far. A little higher. Yes, I think that's it.'

Mama swept a pile of pincushions, lace, and tangled threads to the end of her table and laid out the fabric.

I took a deep breath. I'm always afraid of mentioning my father to Mama, but she was so calm last week on the landing...Perhaps she's finally ready to speak about him.

'Mama, would you tell me a little more about

my father? Just a few small details?'

She froze mid-snip and looked at me in alarm. Then she straightened up, her hand on her throat, scissors pointing at me with their jaws open. 'Well, Martha. What did you want to know?'

The little wings that had sprouted in my heart yesterday fluttered with disbelief. I thought it best to start with something simple. 'Was he very kind?'

Her eyes became glossy and she stared past me, into a world I couldn't see. 'More than you could know, sweetheart. He was the loveliest man in the world. And terribly handsome.'

'And what did he *do*? I mean, you sew, Grandpa Grimstone heals people. And my father? What was his profession?'

'Oh, he was so clever. So gifted with his hands. He…he…' Mama's voice trailed off. The glossiness in her eyes turned to tears, a whole stream that flowed down her face and puddled on the floor at her feet, flooding her shoes. 'I'm sorry, Martha. I can't…I just can't…'

She grasped me fiercely, crushing my face against her bosom. I struggled to breathe. Her tears ran through my plaits and drenched my dress, like a waterfall. Perhaps we won't need rain after all – Mama could cure the drought with her tears.

'Mama,' I tried to say, but I couldn't get out more than a tiny muffled *mmph*. And then suddenly she was gone.

'So clever,' she had said. 'So gifted with his hands. He...he...' He what? Perhaps she had been going to say he created amazing sculptures out of blackstone? Or perhaps she meant he could pick locks with his bare fingers, and sneak into any building he fancied, for he was such a mischievous man. Then I'd know where my own mischief comes from. He handcrafted jewellery with the finest threads of gold? But that doesn't seem right – I'd have seen his creations about the place. He...

The words rang in my head as I changed into a dry dress. It was almost a poem:

So clever. So gifted. He tinkered. His hands...

But it didn't make sense to me.

THURSDAY

I heard the *TING* of the champagne glass by our front door and leaned out the window of the landing. Directly below me was the balding head of Mr Sterling. I groaned, then slid straight down the banister on my stomach, performed a neat flip, and landed on my feet – *my feet! Yes!* I was so pleased with myself I almost forgot to open the front door.

Right. Mr Sterling. The town banker. Last time Frankie Emmerson and I saw him in town, Frankie whispered, 'He uses twenty-pound notes to wipe his derriere when he goes to the outhouse!' We fell over laughing. (Frankie's my friend from the dairy farm down the hill.)

pull string to ring doorbell

Mr Sterling stood there stiffly on our doorstep, his face long as ever, his cheeks hollow. 'Miss Grimstone. I've called to collect my new suit.'

'Oh.' I glanced upwards, but I didn't need any magical gift to see through the ceiling and walls into Mama's sewing studio. I knew perfectly well that the lining of his coat was still laid out on the work table, half cut. The mannequin wore the trousers and shirt, all raw edges and pins. And Mama – she hadn't come to bed last night. She was still in the crypt, weeping over my father.

'Miss Grimstone?'

'Err. I'm sorry, Mr Sterling, but your coat is not quite ready.'

His gloomy face darkened like a storm. 'But that's unacceptable – your mother promised it

today. I'm taking the afternoon train to the city and my old suit has a gaping hole. Let me speak to her, immediately.'

'Err. Umm. Mama's not available

just now,' I told him, stretching my face into its most apologetic smile.

'Fetch her for me regardless. I shall be having words with her about this.'

Well, I didn't know what to do then, for Mama was quite unfetchable, Mr Sterling was glaring at me, and my chest felt tight.

'Grandpa Grimstone!' I yelled, and Mr Sterling stared at me with distaste.

Grandpa must have heard the urgency in my voice, for he was at my side in a moment, a bottle of ground sneefpods open in his hand.

'His suit isn't ready,' I explained. 'And Mr Sterling would have me fetch Mama.'

Grandpa Grimstone understood at once. 'Velvetta is indisposed,' he said firmly. 'She was taken ill in the night and has been unable to complete your suit. She sends her apologies.'

My mouth fell open; I had never heard Grandpa Grimstone tell a lie before. But I was awfully grateful.

'Very well,' said Mr Sterling darkly. He turned on his heel and marched stiffly down the hill from whence he had come.

Grandpa smiled at me kindly, and I seized this opportunity: 'Grandpa Grimstone, will you tell me about my father? I want to know what he was like, what he did...how he died.' (Silence.) 'He was your son! You *must* know. And I'm old enough now, I really am.'

Grandpa stiffened and, like Mama, he looked past me into a world I couldn't see. Whatever he saw saddened him, for he slumped, and his strong old face filled with regret. He lifted his hand as if to dismiss me, but I wasn't giving up so easily.

'IT'S NOT FAIR!'

I yelled, giving him a bit of a start.

Aunt Gertrude barged into the foyer. 'What's all this commotion?'

'Mr Sterling came for his suit, which isn't ready,' Grandpa Grimstone quickly explained.

'Mr Sterling?' Her hands fluttered to her face and her hair. 'Martha, why didn't you tell me Mr Sterling was here?'

'He didn't ask for you. He just wanted his suit.'

'But I always partake of tea with him when he comes.'

It's true she did that – but only once, to my knowledge. I stared at her suspiciously. What does she care about a cup of tea with nasty Mr Sterling? Could it be she has a fancy to marry him? He is a bachelor. But he looks like a grasshopper and his heart is cold and slimy as a river stone!

Aunt Gertrude seemed to come to her senses then, for she turned to me and said sharply, 'Did Mr Sterling pay for the suit?'

I shook my head.

She sighed heavily. 'And now what is to become of us? His remittance was to pay for repairs to the garden fence, the new parlour window, wheat for the quails and the coal bill. Well, now we must pray that someone in the village is taken ill, so that they come and pay for medicine.'

Grandpa Grimstone frowned. 'We'll manage, my dear. If you want to pray for anything, pray for rain, so we can grow some new herbs for my medicines. Just last week I had to turn away Mrs Johnson, for I hadn't any hideosa berries left to give her. That's why our coin jar is empty.'

And then, as if some silent bell had been rung, we all went our separate ways. I lay on my bed and thought about my poor little quails. There was only enough wheat in the sack to feed them for another couple of days.

FRIDAY

Once again I'm supposed to be lessoning myself while Aunt Gertrude attacks apples with the marble chopping board, but I've become distracted. I may have an idea – an invention that could save my quails from starvation...

A Maggot Maker! I know that may sound rather unappealing to you, Dear Diary, but quails *live* for maggots – for them, they're like caviar, to be served on fine silver. I shall draw a plan for my Maggot Maker, fine silver included. I'm sure Aunt Gertrude will think that educational.

Hold on a minute! I just heard a tentative knock at the kitchen door. It swung open and there stood August, brandishing the oddest contraption I've ever seen.

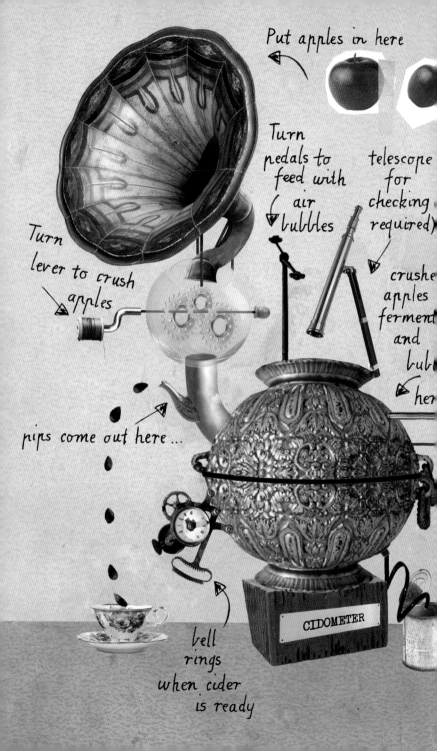

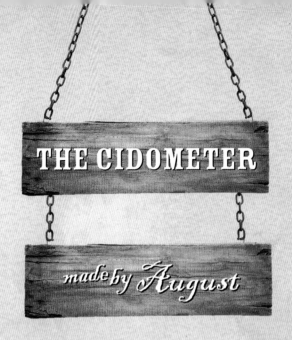

THE CIDOMETER

made by August

turn tap and strain
cider into jug / bottle

old bike wheel to be connected to
pedals to feed air bubbles.

apple cider

le sediment - good for compost
(or would the quails like it?)

'Miss Gertrude,' August said softly, blushing like a boilberry, 'I put this together myself, from bits and pieces I found in the attic. It's to save you the bother of squashing all those apples.'

Aunt Gertrude looked flummoxed. 'I've never heard of such a thing!' she exclaimed. 'Cider, without exception, is produced by hand.'

August slumped. 'As you would, Miss Gertrude. I was only looking to spare your arms.' He set the Cidometer on the kitchen bench and left.

After he'd gone, Aunt Gertrude gave the apples another **WHACK** and the house vibrated again. She rubbed her arms and stared at the machine.

Then she picked up a few apples and poked them tentatively into the mouth of the Cidometer…

SATURDAY

Mama came out of the crypt today. She worked a little on Mr Sterling's suit, but it's still far from finished. August can't do any further maintenance jobs without new supplies, so we're all waiting impatiently, bringing Mama cups of tea and admiring her progress in the hope it will speed things up.

There's only one thornbell left in the garden by the crypt; all the others have withered and died. This morning she was so wilted August gave up his own cup of tea to give her a drink.

She absorbed it gratefully, and lifted her bell-shaped head slightly in appreciation. But August's lips were cracked and dry all day. It seems wrong for Mama to have pot after pot of tea when August hasn't enough, but we're all depending on her now Grandpa has so few herbs left.

With Mama sewing again at last, I could get back to my own plans. I carried Crumpet through the herb garden to the crypt. The thornbell turned to watch us, and the other herbs hissed unhappily as we passed. The crypt walls are built of heavy bluestone, engraved with the words:

Here Lies Mortimer Grimstone

The door is solid oak, with studs that gleam and curling hinges that grasp the wood. I lifted the latch and the door swung open. Cool air fingered our faces, and it smelled of darkness, earth and age.

I set Crumpet on the floor and lifted Mortimer's cloak from the hook on the wall. Mama says it still holds his scent, but all I can smell when I bury my face in the folds of fur, silk and velvet is damp and mustiness. Surely in life my father didn't smell so... *dead*.

I handed Crumpet the cloak. 'There. Now you can work your magic so I can see my father as he was.'

Crumpet stared up at me, his eyes wide.

'Go on!' I urged him. 'Just do the same thing you did in the attic.'

Crumpet fingered the fabric, then turned towards the grave. 'Hpp,' he said, pointing.

'You want me to open it?'

He nodded.

Slowly, I lifted the stone slab. There lay my father, his lashes laced with tiny cobwebs, dust gathering in the creases of his mouth. His hollowed cheeks and pale lips were motionless, as if cast in wax.

Crumpet dragged the cloak to the grave and pushed it over the edge so it slithered onto my father's legs. Then he reached inside, grasping the fabric in both hands.

'Flpph,' he said.

At first nothing happened, and my belly

churned with anxiety. But then slowly, oh so slowly, the cloak rose and hovered above the grave. The dust on my dead father swirled, eddied, and rose up inside the cloak, into an ethereal form of a man. I stared and stared. My father! Made of dust, certainly, but my father all the same!

And then I heard it: a sad, haunting melody, calling me, pulling me. Every note held years of misery, and I was filled with bone-chilling sadness... The pitch rose and there was happiness, too: joy and laughter, bittersweet tears.

I didn't understand this: a music that cradled my whole body and whirled me through a lifetime of emotions. Crumpet had tears on his cheeks. This was no instrument we'd ever heard. It wasn't a piano or a cello, a flute or a bell... but it held power. I closed my eyes, carried on the winds to the bewildering place the music took me.

There was a scent, too, not damp or musty, but something rich and earthy, alive and slightly spicy. I realised that *this* was the smell of my father, warm and comforting.

Crumpet was rustling around, crawling across the crypt to the bronze vase that always stands by the doorway. The vase is really an urn, and one day it will hold my father's ashes, but not yet; Mama isn't ready. Since the drought, she's had to resort to filling it with dry willow stems and hazel branches rather than new roses cut fresh each morning. Crumpet lifted out these twigs and set them on the floor.

With both hands he held up the urn to the dusty form inside the cloak. My father faded, shrinking and swirling as the dark dust that had defined him coiled into the bronze urn, until there was no more.

'No!' I shouted, but it was too late.

My father was gone.

'I wasn't finished!' I cried desperately to Crumpet. 'I need to know how he died, what happened to him. I need to know if he loved me. What you showed me wasn't enough.'

Crumpet lowered his eyes, his tiny lips

trembling. A glassy tear welled on his cheek, and suddenly I was mortified.

'Sorry. I'm sorry! I know you did your best.' I sat beside him and hugged him tightly. He looked up at me with a little smile that somehow told me this wasn't over – not yet.

'Do you…do you know more magic?' I asked, barely daring to hope.

Crumpet pointed at the urn.

'Something about the dust? Can we work magic with that?'

Crumpet nodded.

I brightened. 'What do we do?'

Crumpet slumped and shrugged and shook his head.

I took a slow, deep breath, trying to stay calm. We leaned against the cold bluestone wall for a while in silence, Crumpet hot and still a bit snivelly in my arms.

Suddenly I jumped up. 'Let's go to the apothecary and read the spell books! We'll find what we need, I just *know* it.' Grandpa Grimstone was out, searching the valley with August for herbs somehow untouched by the drought. I know I'm not supposed to go into the apothecary without him, but this was definitely an important way to further Crumpet's magical education, don't you think?

We surveyed the shelves of books. There were piles towering from the floor, books behind books behind books. If only I could somehow pour their contents into my brain,

so that I'd be the all-knowing Magnificent Lady of Magical Spells.

Crumpet disappeared behind a tower of them. 'Geh!' he called.

'This one?' I asked, motioning to a particularly fat tome. He nodded.

We flipped the pages together quickly, until Crumpet stopped us at the one we needed:

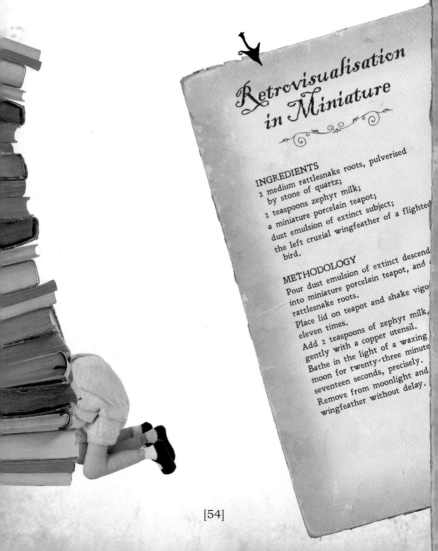

Retrovisualisation in Miniature

INGREDIENTS

2 medium rattlesnake roots, pulverised by stone of quartz;
2 teaspoons zephyr milk;
a miniature porcelain teapot;
dust emulsion of extinct subject;
the left cruxial wingfeather of a flighted bird.

METHODOLOGY

Pour dust emulsion of extinct descend into miniature porcelain teapot, and rattlesnake roots.
Place lid on teapot and shake vigo eleven times.
Add 2 teaspoons of zephyr milk, gently with a copper utensil.
Bathe in the light of a waxing moon for twenty-three minute seventeen seconds, precisely.
Remove from moonlight and wingfeather without delay.

in Miniature

I can see these on the shelves

INGREDIENTS

2 medium rattlesnake roots, pulverised
  by stone of quartz;

2 teaspoons zephyr milk;

a miniature porcelain teapot; There's one in the doll's house

dust emulsion of extinct subject;

the left cruxial wingfeather of a flighted
  bird.

Hmm.

METHODOLOGY

Pour dust emulsion of extinct descendent
into miniature porcelain teapot, and add
rattlesnake roots.

Place lid on teapot and shake vigorously
eleven times.

Add 2 teaspoons of zephyr milk, and stir
gently with a copper utensil.

Bathe in the light of a waxing gibbous
moon for twenty-three minutes and
seventeen seconds, precisely.

Remove from moonlight and add
wingfeather without delay.

when I asked Crumpet what this was, he pointed at the urn.

And then what?

Suddenly we heard the sound of the front door opening.

'Quick! Grandpa Grimstone's back!'

I slammed the book shut, grabbed the urn, hoisted Crumpet onto my hip, and had just made it to the hallway when Grandpa saw us. Although we'd been furthering Crumpet's education, I wasn't quite ready to let Grandpa Grimstone know about my assistance in this matter.

'Look, I found some ficklepods!' Grandpa held up a bunch of greenery. 'I just need to stand them upright to dry, and they'll be ready to use. Oh, this will be perfect for them, thank you.'

He reached for the urn. Crumpet and I looked at each other in alarm. There was a dust emulsion of my dead father inside that urn! But this was not something I was going to mention to Grandpa Grimstone. I couldn't see a single thing I could do but hand it to him.

'There,' he said, placing the urn on the foyer table and arranging the ficklepods inside it. If he'd noticed it was an urn, rather than a vase, he didn't say. Nor did he seem to see the little swirls of dust that rose and sprinkled themselves on the foyer table…

SUNDAY - AFTERNOON

I've been searching for hours for the left cruxial wingfeather of a flighted bird. I looked in all the usual places (the nest in the mulberry tree; under the rock by the creek) and even some unusual places (inside my lovely new letterbox). But no left cruxial wingfeather. Actually, I've a confession to make. I don't know which feather on the left wing is likely to be the cruxial feather. I just hoped I'd know it when I saw it.

I'd thought the bird – the one who follows me everywhere, except when I'm looking for a left cruxial wingfeather – might guide me. But she was nowhere to be seen.

My bevy
of quails

Eventually I went down to the quail pen and found a good-sized feather that was definitely a wingfeather, for it had the right speckles on it. Whether it was left, or cruxial, I couldn't tell. I was also a little worried a quail might not rate as a flighted bird. After all, quails don't normally fly – but thanks to Crumpet's magical words, ours do, these days.

I put the feather in my pocket and decided to hope for the best.

Where are you, bird? ?

MONDAY

It's gone midnight, and the house is sleeping, except for me sitting bolt upright in bed writing in you, Dear Diary.

Mama's asleep beside me, but even when I tried curling against her, listening to the steady beat of her heart and the soft *whoosh* of her breaths, I couldn't sleep.

I wriggled out of Mama's grasp and pulled a snoring Crumpet into my arms, but his comforting weight and warmth couldn't put me to sleep either.

The moon is waxing gibbous, and it's calling me...

FIFTEEN MINUTES LATER

I woke Crumpet and explained I'd collected all the ingredients. He blinked at me, rubbed his eyes, and then pointed towards the apothecary. We picked up the miniature teapot from the doll's house on the landing, and went to the foyer to get the urn. I laid the ficklepods on the foyer table, and Crumpet blew a little puff of air that made the dust rise from the table and stems of the ficklepods and swirl back into the urn – thankfully.

I will tell you the rest JUST as it happened to us, Dear Diary…so you can feel precisely as I did as each moment unfolded.

It's a busy place, the apothecary, even in the dark of night, with small creatures flying and chittering, a box that wails, and books that flutter their pages until Grandpa Grimstone sets them aright in the morning. But as I tiptoe in, Crumpet blows through his lips and moves his hands this way and that until everything stills. I light a candle, and the remaining croaks and groans and scuffles fade away as the room comes into focus. My heart is beating much too hard, my breath is short, and I swear, if Crumpet wasn't so confident, I'd flee back to my bed.

Crumpet motions to me. I'm to fetch the rattlesnake roots and the zephyr milk. Next I remove the lid of the teapot, and Crumpet picks up the urn. He tips it carefully and the dust swirls out, billowing, then sucking itself into the tiny porcelain pot. I add the rattlesnake roots.

Clamping the lid tightly onto the teapot, I shake it vigorously, eleven times, exactly.

Crumpet measures in the zephyr milk, and I stir it oh-so-softly with Grandpa Grimstone's copper owl spoon.

'Thank you,' I whisper to the owl. Then Crumpet and I both turn to the window to look at the moon.

I lift the latch, and the window answers me noisily as I open it.

I glance at the clock as Crumpet places the teapot, lid off, on the sill. The moon bathes it with an eerie white glow.

What are we going to do for the next twenty-three minutes and seventeen seconds? I take the speckled quail feather from the pocket of my nightdress and hand it to Crumpet.

His eyes widen in alarm, and he shakes his head vehemently.

'This is not the left cruxial wingfeather of a flighted bird?' I ask him.

Clearly, it is not. Crumpet crawls across the room and motions to a book high on one of Grandpa Grimstone's shelves.

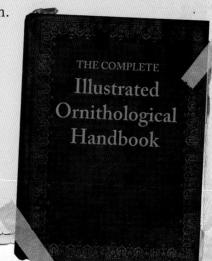

THE COMPLETE Illustrated Ornithological Handbook

I lift it down.

Warning: don't use this device to reach sponge cakes

We pore over the drawings of birds – but if the word 'cruxial' is somewhere between the covers, it does not reveal itself to us.

Thirteen minutes and twenty-eight seconds left.

'The quail pen?' I suggest, and Crumpet nods.

Even the quail pen creaks at night, casting big loomy shadows over the birds, their perches rattling slightly in the wind. I lift the fattest quail from her perch and she looks around groggily, blinking in surprise. I set her on my lap and spread her left wing. 'O Cruxial Feather! Speak to me!' I command. But no feather speaks. One of them does seem longer than the others, and I eye it off, but Crumpet is shaking his head again. I return the quail to her perch.

Six minutes and nineteen seconds.

Crumpet makes a flapping motion with his hands.

'I know,' I told him. 'I've been looking everywhere for the bird. But she hasn't been around lately. Shall we try the mulberry tree?'

Crumpet points to his lips.

'Good idea!' I sing my bird's very favourite song, the one that always draws her to peck at my bread when I'm carrying it home from the village.

Three minutes and eleven seconds.

No sign of the bird.

'Maybe we should just try it with the feather we have,' I suggest. 'The magic *might* work.'

Crumpet nods, but I can see he's not convinced.

We trudge back to the apothecary, and with just four seconds to go, Crumpet lifts the speckled feather and holds it ready.

Precisely twenty-three minutes and seventeen seconds after we set it on the sill, I lift the teapot and whisk it back to shadow. Crumpet is lowering the speckled feather when a sharp breeze beats suddenly against my face.

Silhouetted against the moon is my bird!

She flies towards us, wings beating hard, and curls her claws around the windowsill. She spreads her left wing, and reaches with her beak to pluck not the longest feather but a sturdier one just beneath it. Knocking the speckled quail feather aside, she reaches towards the teapot and presses her wingfeather through the tiny opening. We all stare at the feather poking out of the teapot's top. It shimmers for a moment, then turns to dust, sucked into the tiny pot.

The bird spreads her wings, but instead of disappearing into the night she flutters awkwardly to the floor. That's when I realise her sacrifice: she'll need to grow a new cruxial wingfeather before she can fly again.

'Thank you, little bird, *thank you*,' I whisper. I set her on my shoulder.

A BIT LATER STILL

We're on the landing now. I perch the bird on the doll's house roof; she takes the teapot from Crumpet with her beak and tilts the spout above the chimney. The dust pours down into the doll's house, transforming into a gleaming blue liquid as it does so, thicker than water, smoother than honey. No matter how much the bird pours, there's more – more and more – more than the little teapot could possibly hold. It flows down the chimney and out through the fireplace in the parlour, filling the room, the entire doll's house, as though it were a pool, bubbles writhing in the corners.

As Crumpet and I watch through the windows, the liquid turns to air, and a cold sapphire glow emanates from the doll's house, lighting the landing more powerfully than any candle could. I lift the bird back to my shoulder so that she can watch, too.

The doll's house is a mess: the furniture still fallen from our storm game, the dolls toppled everywhere. But as the liquid turns to light and swirls around the man doll, he stands up. And he changes: his moustache fades to nothing, his limbs grow longer, his round belly presses flat. Even the features on his face shift, until I recognise him as my father.

Furniture settles itself, until the house is neat and tidy. In the bedroom is a cradle I've never seen before, and sitting amongst the quilts is a tiny girl with short black plaits. I know her as well as I know myself.

'That's me!' I whisper to Crumpet. He smiles, his eyes shiny with delight, and wriggles sideways to sit in my lap.

The Mortimer doll walks to the apothecary, but he doesn't move stiffly like the dolls we've played with before. Now he really *is* my father, made tiny by Crumpet's magic.

The grandpa doll has become my own grand-father, somehow younger, brisker and brimming with energy.

He's showing Mortimer a spell in his book, directing him around the apothecary, leaning over to correct his work. And then I get it:

Grandpa Grimstone is teaching Mortimer to work magic!

But something's wrong.

Mortimer steps back, shaking his head, motioning towards the ceiling.

'He doesn't want to learn!' I whisper.

Grandpa Grimstone insists, but Mortimer is pleading, refusing. He escapes and races upstairs. Grandpa stomps about crossly, slamming a book closed, storming outside and casting his eyes to the heavens.

Upstairs, Mortimer plucks the baby Martha from her cradle and rocks her in his arms, smoothing her hair (my hair!) against his chest, pacing the room.

'He's trying to put me to sleep.'

But the baby isn't sleeping. She keeps

popping up,
laughing,

batting his face with her hands
when he shushes her.

[75]

Mortimer fetches something. It's…what's that? It's not a harp, but it reminds me of one: a beautiful stringed instrument on wheels, almost as tall as Mortimer, with a velvet seat built into its frame, like the heel of a shoe – Crumpet's horse-seat from the attic! He settles the instrument by the cradle and begins to play.

At once I recognise the sad, haunting melody from the crypt. Softly now, it echoes against the windows of the doll's house, but it still brings tears to my cheeks. The baby, me, she lies down, lulled by the music. 'He's playing for *me*.'

In my head I hear Mama's trembling voice. 'So gifted with his hands. He…he…' He played this strange instrument! The harp that's not a harp.

I'm jolted from my thoughts when the storm detector in the doll's house apothecary suddenly wails and flashes its warning. Crumpet and I stare at each other. A storm is coming! A doll's-house-sized storm.

Mortimer instantly stops playing and hurries downstairs. Me, the little me in the cradle, I'm still awake, watching him go.

Next thing, Grandpa Grimstone and Mortimer are arguing. They peer anxiously out at the sky. Grandpa Grimstone gestures to the spell book, and Mortimer shakes his head, emphatically.

'I think Mortimer really doesn't want to do magic,' I whisper.

Grandpa Grimstone mimes Mortimer playing the harp-like instrument. His eyes roll skywards, and with his hands he dismisses the vision. It's perfectly clear what he's saying: 'Stop fooling around with music and apply yourself to serious business.' He wants Mortimer to cast a spell to protect the valley from the storm; I recognise those books, that particular collection of jars. But Mortimer has something else on his mind...me. He glances upwards.

Next moment, the doll's house is plunged into darkness. I gasp and grab onto Crumpet tighter than ever. He squirms in my grip. The bird's claws dig into my shoulder. Lightning flashes:

dark, light, dark, light.

And suddenly I remember! I remember that night, with perfect clarity: it's as if I'm lying in my cradle again! When the thunder cracked, fear flooded my body and I pulled myself up on the railing, flailed and fell, tumbling to the floor. Lightning flashed through the room, turning everything on its head – or perhaps it was *me* turned on *my* head? – and I groped and crawled until I found a safe space. Under Mama's bed, perhaps? It was warm and still and dark, and I could barely hear the thunder. Confused but safe, I closed my eyes and imagined Pappi's music.

Pappi. I was too little to speak, but I called him Pappi.

Now the doll's house is lit again, and there's Mortimer, hurrying up the stairs. Oh no, the cradle's empty! He rushes around the room, opening and closing cupboards, crawling under furniture. Where did the baby go?

Crumpet points to the front door of the doll's house. There's my mama, Velvetta, arriving home, a basket on her arm and her shawl all askew from the wind.

She finds Mortimer panicked, dashing up and down the stairs, peering into every crevice in the house. When Velvetta realises what he's searching for, she drops her basket and searches, too. In the apothecary, Grandpa Grimstone bends over his cauldron, working the spells I've seen him cast during every storm since.

'Look in the cupboard, under the bed. Or behind the dresser. I'm there. I *know* I'm there,' I whisper through the bedroom window. But Mortimer and Velvetta can't hear me. They stop in the hall, breathing hard.

He's gesturing outside, wanting to search out there. Velvetta is shaking her head; it's too dangerous! But in the end she has no choice. They think I could be out there, unprotected. She nods. Fumbling with the clasp at her throat, she hands him her cloak. A hole gapes in it, right over his heart, and Velvetta pinches it closed. You can see she wants to fix it right there and then – but of course there's no time.

Cloak unfastened, hole gaping, Mortimer opens the door to the storm. Wind strikes him in the face, blowing his hair on end. Rain splatters the foyer. Velvetta is forced back against the stairs and Mortimer steps over the threshold.

Grandpa Grimstone hurries into the foyer, looking for Mortimer. Velvetta points at the door and Grandpa's face changes: he's relieved, delighted even.

I nudge Crumpet. 'He thinks Mortimer's gone to fight the storm. He doesn't realise the baby is missing.'

Suddenly the storm isn't just inside the doll's house; it's on the landing, too. I can feel the wind hurling against my skin. My plaits beat against my neck, and my nightie billows out. My skin prickles with goosebumps. The bird's feathers ruffle against my cheek.

I clutch Crumpet even closer and peer through the bedroom window. And there's Velvetta, pulling the baby Martha out from the pile of blankets behind the chest! I remember this, too: the comforting rose perfume of my mama, mixed with her sweat and fear. She cradled me against her, kissing the bump on my forehead and rocking me gently. Finally, I closed my eyes. My baby world was set to rights when I was in Mama's arms.

But, watching through the window now, I can see that Velvetta's world is not right. She peers out into the night, then she glances back at me, obviously torn – should she brave the storm herself to find Mortimer? Or stay with the baby?

She stays.

Lightning cracks again and the bedroom goes dark. I can see only the outside of the doll's house now, its shingled roof lit up in flashes, the tree painted on the outside wall suddenly blowing and gusting until it's no longer attached to the doll's house at all. It's uprooted and hurled to the ground by the raging wind.

'There's Mortimer!' I hiss. He's been lifted by the wind and has landed on all fours – on the roof!

He calls out something. I know just the words he will be using:

> ... galeo trans meridian
>   quasi-mercurial nadir
> dispatch castellanus
>   via celestial perehelion ...'

There's a lull in the wind, and my nightdress settles against my side as Mortimer stands up. Yes! *He's going to beat the storm*, I think. *He did learn enough magic to do this!*

But the wind seethes, and suddenly Mortimer is blown free, in a spiral around the doll's house. Arms flailing, legs kicking, he grabs the roof, but a shingle comes off. He grabs the gutter, but it slips away. He crashes into the chimney and clings to it.

'Go inside!' I call to him frantically, but he doesn't hear me. I reach out a hand. I'll pick him up, hold him safe against my chest. Crumpet pulls me back. His message is clear: we watch but must not touch.

...of aleutian low
precipitate to Northern aphelion
azores atmospheric ...

The wind lulls again and there is quiet. Mortimer climbs unsteadily to the top of the chimney, blood on his forehead, his trousers gashed. He raises his arms commandingly to the heavens, and summons every tiny bit of the magic he knows to banish the storm.

He's going to win, to cast away the terrible weather, even without potions to help! But no. The storm roars directly overhead. Lightning sizzles across the doll's house. An arrow of lightning shoots towards Mortimer, straight through the hole in his cloak and into his heart. I see it clearly, in slow motion. He is struck motionless, his arms outstretched, and then he's falling, falling, tossing and whirling, until he lands on the ground, his body flopped awkwardly, completely still.

The wind gathers itself, coiling upwards, taking the lightning and thunder with it, up, up to the landing ceiling, and then it's gone.

My ears ring with silence and stillness. My nightdress hangs limp. Crumpet lets out a long, slow breath, and I remember to breathe, too.

By the doll's house, the little Velvetta rushes to Mortimer and hurls herself over him. A keening sound, a long, slow note of tragedy, rings through the landing. She lays her cheek on his heart and sobs.

I understand now: *Mama thinks Mortimer's death is her fault.*

The sobbing rises in my chest, too, and tears run down my face, though I barely knew him.

Perhaps I grieve for Mama, for all that she has lost, for the guilt she carries. Or perhaps for the silence Mortimer has left behind, where his haunting melody used to be.

Slowly, Grandpa Grimstone makes his way from the doll's house to kneel before Mortimer. He cups his son's cheek with his hand.

'I'm sorry … I'm so sorry,' Grandpa seems to be saying. 'You didn't have the gift; I shouldn't have forced you. I should have listened when you told me you were made for music, not magic…'

And that's when I know that Grandpa Grimstone, too, feels guilt for Mortimer's death. He doesn't know that my father went out into the storm to search for me.

Crumpet holds out the teapot and lays it next to Mortimer. He blows gently, a little puff of air, and suddenly the tiny Mortimer turns to dust.

'Not yet!' I whisper to Crumpet. But again it's too late. The dust swirls and eddies in its own tiny storm, and is sucked into the teapot. Crumpet clutches it to his chest.

'Ipt,' he says.

JUST BEFORE DAWN

The pale light of dawn was rising over the valley as I carried Crumpet, the bird and the teapot to the crypt. I felt calm, washed clean. The herbs in the garden hung their heads quietly, in respect, as though we were a funeral procession bringing my father home.

We lifted the stone slab and Crumpet poured the dust from the teapot into the grave. The dust glimmered and fell thickly, swirling to fill every crevice. For a moment, my father's body was illuminated with a ghostly glow. But then he faded and the dust settled into the cracks around him.

Solemnly, I bowed my head. 'Goodnight, Pappi.'

Next stop was the mulberry tree, where I lifted the bird into her nest, whispering my thanks and promising to look after her until she could fly again.

I checked the apothecary and tidied away the last traces of our magic, lest Grandpa Grimstone discover our secret. We returned the urn to the table in the foyer, and arranged the ficklepods just as they had been.

I could hear the world stirring: the first rustle

of feathers from the quail pen; the early sigh of petals opening for the day.

Crumpet felt heavy in my weary arms. It wasn't easy to carry him back up the stairs. The doll's house on the landing looked as it always had, with the tree painted on its side, and the dolls neatly lined up in the parlour.

Mama is waking now. Time for me to hide this diary and close my eyes.

TUESDAY NIGHT

I slept all day.

I dreamed and dreamed of my father. In my dream he was holding me in his arms and I could smell him, warm and spicy and familiar. His lullaby rocked me and I felt something I've never felt before: whole, safe and content. No, that's not true: I've felt this before, back when I was a baby and Pappi was alive. But I'd forgotten it was possible.

To think I've been walking around all this time as if I were complete and fine, when really there were nasty jagged cracks all through my bones I didn't even know were there. Those cracks spilled out all the inside goodness and made me somehow hollow, leaving a gap inside me that kept wanting to be filled.

In my dream the blue liquid that filled the doll's house flooded my body through the cracks, and filled me up so there were no gaps. I was whole again. And as soon as I woke, I knew what that blue liquid was. It was my father's love for me, bubbling all through me! He loved me!

Not only did Pappi love me, back when I was uncracked and little, but he braved the storm to look for me. He *died* looking for me.

My Dearest Diary,

perhaps this sounds crazy,

but I think that

blue liquid truly is healing my bones,

now I know I really and truly

was loved.

And not only that —

wherever my father has gone

(and I'm not talking about his body, which

lies cold and waxy in the crypt),

I think his love for me

might still be there — I can picture him

floating somewhere in the sky, waiting to

release that blue liquid onto me,

to spill it

down

like rain-

drops.

I'm so tired. I'm going back to sleep. Every time I close my eyes I can see my father's fingers, spinning across that magnificent harp-like instrument he played, and I can hear his music, too faint to take me someplace else, but beautiful nonetheless.

Wednesday

Martha Grimstone
The Bedroom at the
top of the stairs

Dear Mama,

I'm so glad you didn't go out into the storm to fetch Pappi. You would have died, too, and I would be an orphan now. Even if you are very busy sewing all the time, I still need you as my mama. You mustn't blame yourself for Pappi's death. It isn't anyone's fault that he died — it was just a terrible accident.

I'm sorry I upset you by asking about him. But I hope someday you'll tell me more about him, when you're ready.

All my love,

Your daughter,

Martha Grimstone

Wednesday

Martha Grimstone
The Bedroom at the
top of the stairs

Dear Grandpa Grimstone,

Please don't ask how I found this out, but
I know what happened the night my father
died. Mortimer didn't go out into the
storm to fight it, or to prove his skills in
magic. He went out looking for me, because
I was lost. He tried to protect himself, but
he couldn't. It's not your fault he died. If
anything, it's mine, though I don't think
you really can blame a baby for what
happened.

I also know why you won't teach me
magic. You think you shouldn't have tried

to train someone who wasn't gifted in that way. But let me tell you one thing — I'm sure I do have a gift, and you should teach me as well as Crumpet.

Yours in readiness to learn,

Martha Grimstone

FRIDAY

First thing this morning, Crumpet and I went down to the quail pen to see if any maggots had hatched. We'd been checking daily, but there'd been none so far.

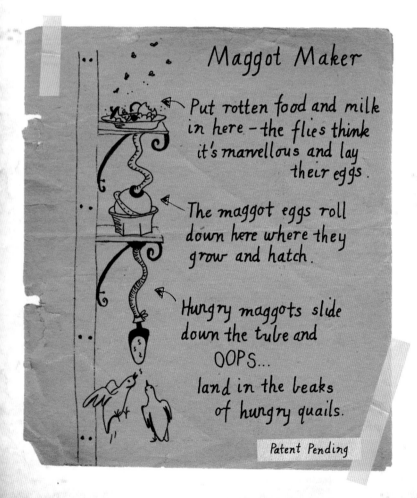

Maggot Maker

Put rotten food and milk in here – the flies think it's marvellous and lay their eggs.

The maggot eggs roll down here where they grow and hatch.

Hungry maggots slide down the tube and OOPS... land in the beaks of hungry quails.

Patent Pending

You can't expect instant results with a Maggot Maker, as it takes a while for the maggots to hatch and find their way down the ramp, but once the first makes its journey the others will follow. Maggots do like a good game of Follow the Leader.

Sure enough, this morning I came down to find the *very first* maggot, falling straight into the beak of our biggest, fattest quail. I witnessed the second, third and fourth maggots also tumble into the very same beak, while the other quails stood around watching longingly.

I glared at the fat quail. 'You'll go straight to the chopping block if you don't learn to share.'

The fat quail glared back at me and ate the fifth maggot.

Crumpet was far more effective. 'Da,' he said, and the quails started marching in a neat figure eight. The littlest quail stopped directly under the Maggot Maker. When she had eaten a maggot, they all marched to the next spot, and another quail stood in the eating spot.

'Miss Martha? I have something to show you, if you will.'

Crumpet and I turned to look up at August.

'To the attic,' he said, and we followed, delivering a few maggots to the bird in the mulberry tree on the way.

In the attic I stopped short, for there, by the trapdoor, was the oddest thing. It had a frame that was taller than me and wide as two doors. It was built from a hodgepodge of brass crossbows with multiple strings, giant metallic boomerangs, a bronze wheel, and strings tied this way and that, held taut with pale bone knobs of all sizes and shapes.

'Do you like it, Miss Martha? I've been trying to put together some of the things Mortimer made. But I'm stumped – I can't work out what to do with these.'

He pointed to a pile of knobs, strings, and little golden bells tangled around a bronze wheel on the floor. 'I think I know where these extra bits go,' I said.

An hour later, there was just one thing left on the floor: a small brass plate. I turned it over.

So that was what he'd called it, this magnificent instrument, the harp that's not a harp. The Epithium!

Now I understood that my father had a gift – a gift with his hands, both to craft this exquisite thing, and to bring forth music from it.

I laid my cheek against its frame, which was cool, smooth and welcoming. Gingerly, I seated myself on the plush velvet cushion and leaned forwards. I ran my fingers across the strings and they chimed for me, light and delighted, like bubbles filling the attic.

I closed my eyes, and something magical happened. My fingers moved, pulling this string and that one, reaching high here and low there, and with each note I played they shifted a little, learned a little, knew better what to do – more this way, further that way – until I was playing a melody. Not just any melody, I realised, but the very same one I'd heard in the crypt.

The music filled every part of my being, lifting me so I felt I was being rocked on an enormous ocean. Time rushed through me, and I felt again every sadness I'd had in my life, every ache, every tear; then it changed, whooshing upwards until I was so happy I thought I would explode. There was sweetness in my mouth, tears in my lashes, and when I couldn't bear it anymore, I opened my eyes.

I started with shock. For there, in the attic, stood Mama. Drawn by my father's music, she came and she stayed, instead of running away to the crypt.

I met her eyes, but only for an instant, because right behind her was Grandpa Grimstone. He was dabbing at his face with a handkerchief, steadying himself on the head of an old, broken rocking horse. Beside him, August swayed to my music. And behind them all was the sturdy dark shape of Aunt Gertrude.

As I played my final notes a strong breeze blew in, and I saw that rain clouds had gathered overhead. I ran my fingers across the strings one last time, then rested my hands in my lap.

There was a silence so long that the attic throbbed with waiting.

At last Mama said,

'Oh Martha. You've inherited your father's gift.'

'I never thought I'd hear Mortimer's melody again,'

Grandpa Grimstone added.

'I'd thought the valley would be silent of his music forever.'

FRIDAY

This morning I was pretend-scowling over my Latin at the kitchen table, but really thinking about music. In the two weeks since we put together the Epithium, I've practised on it every day after my lessons.

The thing I like best about my practice is this: at that time of day, Crumpet is with Grandpa Grimstone learning magic, Mama is sewing, Aunt Gertrude is busy in the kitchen, August is tending the herbs, and I, Martha Grimstone, am also hard at work doing something just as vital and magnificent.

The thing I like second-best is that with every passing day there is more music in my fingers and I can play faster, more complicated melodies.

Last week I discovered a box filled with hand-written music worksheets in the attic – Mortimer's own notes! It took me a good while just to learn how to read his rough scrawl. Once I'd done that, I had to work out what it all meant. Clearly, my father couldn't write as fast as he could think. For example by *Mst inv poss impct of mldy in lwr reg*

I think he meant 'Must investigate possible impact of melody in a lower register'. Slowly, I came to understand that my father had been working on something

I was just starting to strum my fingers and hum one of his tunes this morning when Mama swished into the room.

'Finished!' she announced, holding up Mr Sterling's new suit.

Aunt Gertrude straightened up immediately from the tray of quail-egg pastries she was making for the solstice party. 'Martha, we must make deliverance of the suit immediately. August could attend to the parlour window if we were to acquire the glass hitherto.'

Aunt Gertrude hardly ever lets me skip my lessons, so I closed my book and stood up before she could change her mind. She usually sends me to deliver Mama's garments on my own, if we are so desperate for money that we can't wait for them to be picked up. But apparently a visit to Mr Sterling justified cancelling the entire day's work – even when it was the day before summer solstice.

Aunt Gertrude changed into her best day-dress, arranged her hair so it looked like octopus tentacles, and wrapped Mr Sterling's suit in brown paper.

We walked to town together, the bird on my shoulder for the outing, me clicking my fingers and kicketying my heels to make a fine rhythm while Aunt Gertrude muttered how nice it would be if one could only hear the breeze and the birds. The bird joined my tune, singing loudly.

Even though she could now hear said bird, Aunt Gertrude frowned. Truly, there's no pleasing my aunt!

But she smiled with approval when she opened the gate in Mr Sterling's white picket fence. 'Look at that lovely border of flowers. Oh, for a garden where the snapdragons don't snap at me as I walk past.'

Well, I thought the flowers looked very ordinary indeed, compared to what grows around our place.

'If I lived here I'd never need fret about money

again. I could keep this house in perfect repair,' Aunt Gertrude said wistfully.

I know she didn't exactly choose to live with us. Grandpa Grimstone sent for her when my father died, as Mama was so miserable with grief she never left the crypt, even for a moment. Someone was needed to run the house and look after me. But we're too eccentric for Aunt Gertrude. And too poor.

Mr Sterling answered the door frostily. 'It's fortunate you caught me,' he said by way of hello. 'I was returning to the bank. You really should see me there if you wish me to look after your money.'

As if we *had* any money to look after!

Aunt Gertrude blushed and fingered her octopus tentacles. 'Good morning, Mr Sterling. We've come to deliver your suit.' She held out the brown paper package.

Mr Sterling glared at it. 'It's too late. I needed it for my trip to the city the other week.'

'I believe my uncle

informed you Velvetta was incapacitated. It couldn't be helped, and she's most apologetic.'

'Nevertheless, I won't be paying. A deal is a deal, and she broke it. My mother held a ball in my honour, to introduce me to eligible young ladies. And I had to greet them in my scruffy old suit.'

Aunt Gertrude flinched. I knew how much *she* would have liked to go to that ball. 'Velvetta expended hours on this suit! It was bespoke. You are obligated to pay!'

'Good day to you, Miss Grimstone.' And with that, Mr Sterling closed the door firmly in our faces.

For a moment I thought Aunt Gertrude would cry. Then she sniffed, pulled her chin up high, and led me out the gate. 'You know, Martha, I think those flowers look insipid. I wouldn't reside here if you paid me to do so!'

'Me neither,' I agreed, and I took the offending package from Aunt Gertrude so she wouldn't have to carry it home.

But what will we do with it now? And how will we fix the parlour window?

SATURDAY - SUMMER SOLSTICE

At first we thought we'd have to cancel our party. But Grandpa Grimstone said it wasn't fair to call it off at such short notice, when the villagers had already bathed and started dressing in their finest clothes. Parlour window or no, the party must go on.

'I put the Epithium in front of the boards,' said August, 'so's everyone will be too busy admiring it to even notice the window.'

The champagne glass TINGed, and I opened the door to the first of our guests.

I heard Mama say, 'August, those overalls won't do. Take this package – you're about the same size as Mr Sterling.'

The Emmersons were first to arrive, then the Johnsons, the Fifes, the vicar… Soon almost everyone from the village had gathered in our parlour. The champagne glass TINGed again, and this time I found Mr Sterling standing beside a very glamorous lady. She had long white hair coiled on top of her head, and was adorned with more jewels than I've ever seen.

'I present my mother, Lady Sterling, who is visiting me from the city,' said Mr Sterling.

Lady Sterling smiled and inclined her head graciously. I dropped an awkward little curtsey, though I never normally curtsey to anyone.

'I'm delighted to meet you, child.' She reached out and touched one of my plaits. 'You've such lovely hair. I always wished for dark plaits like these.' To Mr Sterling, she said, 'What an amazing house! Look at those portraits – I'm sure they were painted by Mortrause. I've always admired his work. Oh! Do you really have ficklepods here?' She bent over the urn on the occasional table. 'I can never get these in the city.'

'We grow them here in the valley,' I said shyly. 'Though they aren't doing too well just now, because of the drought.'

I led them to the parlour, where everyone was milling around, chatting and accepting hors d'oeuvres from a large platter August was offering around. Lady Sterling took a small pastry, then she put her arm around my shoulder and whispered, 'Who is that well dressed man?'

'That's August.' I was about to add, 'He's the gardener,' but that didn't sound glamorous, so I said, 'His family has worked here for many generations. My mother sewed his suit.'

'Really?' Lady Sterling turned to her son. 'Did you hear that, Furchell? You should order one just like it. Finely tailored indeed. You would look most handsome in such a suit.'

Before Mr Sterling could respond, the tinkling of a bell rang through the house. Everyone stopped talking and looked around questioningly.

'What was that?'

'The Cidometer!' August exclaimed. 'The cider be ready.'

'Excuse me,' I murmured to Lady Sterling, and raced to the kitchen.

Sparkling golden cider ran from the Cidometer tap into Aunt Gertrude's glass. She took a sip, swallowed cautiously, then gave the biggest smile of her life.

'This is undoubtedly the most delectable cider I've ever had!' She handed the glass to August, who blushed and sipped from the very place where her lips had been.

He held up the glass and bowed low. 'Miss Gertrude, you have just made the best cider ever to grace this valley.'

'Why, no, August. It was, uh, it was you,' Aunt Gertrude stammered, unused to giving compliments. 'It was the contraption you devised.'

Trays of cider were presented to our guests. The mood became very merry indeed as everyone drained glass after glass of the exquisite liquid, and marvelled at August's modern invention. Aunt Gertrude blushed with pride when August insisted that only her delicate touch could have coaxed such a perfect drink from it.

I saw Grandpa Grimstone slipping the last of his remaining pots of ointment into people's hands and knew Aunt Gertrude would soon politely collect their money. And Mama was inundated with requests for a suit just like the one August was wearing. If anyone noticed the boarded-up window, they didn't mention it.

As Mama swept past me, her arm linked with the wife of a man who I knew would soon be wearing a fine new suit, she paused to slide something into my hand. By the time I'd glanced down at the folded slip of paper, Mama had vanished. Inching into the corner, I unfolded the note:

from the sewing table
of Velvetta Grimstone

My dear Martha,
There's no way I would have gone into the storm to fetch Mortimer. I knew I couldn't leave you, Martha, not while there was a raging storm to terrify you.

No – I felt it was my fault because I didn't sew up the hole in the cloak. If only I'd <u>made him wait</u>, and sewn it up right there and then.

With love, Your mama,
Velvetta Grimstone

Tears came to my eyes as I realised something. My mama loves me just as much as my father did. I had thought, Dear Diary, that she couldn't love me all *that* much, as she's always too busy and distracted to be much of a mama. But now I see that she, too, is suffering from all those cracks in her bones, without Mortimer here to keep us whole.

Grandpa Grimstone hadn't said anything about his note. I slipped through the crowd until I found him speaking in a low voice to Mrs Fife, gesturing to a red rash she had on her neck. I waited until Mrs Fife turned away, then grasped his hand.

'Grandpa? Did you read my letter?'

'Yes, Martha.' He paused for ever so long, but finally turned his eyes to me. 'I did eventually learn you'd gone missing in the storm. Velvetta told me. But until then, I did think it was my fault Mortimer died.'

He squeezed my fingers, and we both watched August offer Mrs Fife a cider from the tray.

'I made a grave mistake,' Grandpa said, 'trying to teach Mortimer. I should have listened to him. I should have listened to myself. I knew, deep down, that magic was not his calling, but I ignored it because I longed to leave my work to someone who could carry on our family tradition.'

'The Epithium?' Lady Sterling's voice rang through the room. 'What an intricate construction! Does anyone here play? I should very much like to hear it.'

Grandpa Grimstone placed his hands on my shoulders. 'I'm sure Martha would play for you, dear lady.'

As I sat down on the red velvet seat, all eyes were on me. My heart pounded, my stomach swarmed with beetles, and I thought perhaps I might faint. But I managed to steady my nerves, and I began to play my favouritest of Mortimer's melodies...It is <u>achingly difficult</u>, but each time I play it my hands move more quickly and confidently, and the music seems to grow more powerful.

Now, there is something

VERY IMPORTANT

I have not yet told you, Dear Diary. I have made the most magnificent discovery, a huge secret about my father's music, known only to him, closely guarded within cryptic notations on his worksheets...

HE USED HIS MUSIC TO COMMAND THE WEATHER.

Yes! With just the right melody, Mortimer Grimstone could bring rain! He could bring sunshine, breezes, and adjust the skies in delicate ways that gave the perfect balance needed by the herbs in our valley. Sometimes he could even turn back the early makings of a storm. And he was working up music **SO POWERFUL** it could stop a full-blown storm in its tracks, like Grandpa Grimstone's spell...though that music sheet was incomplete.

In fact, it was dated the very day of his death.

As my music filled the room now, everyone began to sway. Mr Fife tapped his foot, and Frankie Emmerson jigged in front of me. August bowed to

Aunt Gertrude and held out his hand. I thought she might slap him, but instead she placed her hand delicately in his. They danced, whirling around the parlour, as my fingers moved deftly over the strings. The beetles in my stomach settled, and I played better, faster, more powerfully than ever before.

Lady Sterling whispered loudly to her son, 'Perhaps you could court Miss Gertrude. She seems a fine maiden. And if you marry into this charming family, we can drink her cider all year long!'

But I had a feeling Aunt Gertrude wouldn't be interested, for her cheeks were pink and her head was thrown back with laughter. Her octopus-tentacle curls had loosened into a lovely cascade down her back, and I could see why Lady Sterling thought she looked so fine. August spun her fast, then grasped her waist and dipped her into a deep arch. He leaned down, his lips about to touch hers …

when …

'IT'S RAINING!'

Frankie Emmerson shouted.

And it was! The rain clouds that had gathered, seeming darker and darker each time I played this melody, had finally

OPE NED

and water poured from the sky.

Blue
liquid
bubbled

into ponds and lakes
on the ground,

filling all the cracks of the earth.

Through the windowpane that wasn't boarded up, I could see the herbs stretching and reaching for the water, swelling as they drank.

'This is like having Mortimer with us again!' Mrs Emmerson exclaimed. 'I would hear him practising his music each morning while I was milking the cows. How I've missed that boy.' She smiled at me fondly. 'Now my cows will fatten and we'll have milk again.'

The villagers cheered as I played on. Suddenly the windowpane darkened and I saw a beautiful sight: the silhouette of my bird as she flew past. At last her cruxial wingfeather had regrown.

I felt my moment of magnificence had arrived:

Lady Martha the Magnificent.

The End

The Making of the Grimstones

Dear Reader,

I made the family of Grimstone puppets myself, and furnished their miniature home. This was for my gothic theatre show, *The Grimstones*. It took me eighteen months to handcraft everything, mostly from recycled junk. They were some of the happiest days of my life, because nothing gives me more pleasure than making things with my own hands.

Since my partner, Paula Dowse, and I began performing with the Grimstones, as puppeteers and narrators for the show, we have toured Australia and the world. It seems that, like me, our audiences have fallen in love with my little puppet family.

Between shows, Martha Grimstone sits on her tiny bed and scrawls in her notebook, unleashing all the excitements and frustrations of her everyday life. Her words are captivating, her little drawings so enchanting, that I

can't help myself from sharing them with you. Every time I take one of her notebooks I leave an empty one in its place, and she winks at me, because Martha longs to be famous and can't wait for you to read her diary!

If you would like to know more about the Grimstones, please visit **www.thegrimstones.com**. You can watch them come to life on YouTube, download beautiful photos of their miniature world, and see where they'll be performing next. Find the Grimstones on Facebook, follow them on Twitter, and read my blog.

Online, you can also order *The Grimstones – An Artist's Journal,* which records my creative process while making the Grimstones puppets and show, from my initial spark of an idea through to a theatrical production that has toured the world. It's jam-packed with sketches, beautiful photographs and 'how to' tips, providing inspiration to create and bring more creativity into your life.

Thank you for sharing the Grimstones with me.

Love and creative fire to you!

THE GRIMSTONES

HATCHED

My first diary—lots of secrets inside!
All about Crumpet !!

Martha Grimstone longs to cure Mama of her lake
of tears, and find a real friend at last. If only she
could get into Grandpa Grimstone's apothecary
and work her very own spell…

Make sure you read
the first book in
The Grimstones series –
and watch out
for more from
Martha Grimstone!